CW01020462

# CONTENTS

*Chapter 1:*

*Like A Dream*

It's bitterly cold. The wind is strong and frigid. Every time it blows past me, I shudder and feel cold, icy chills run down my back. The sky is a mix of two colors, and both are so pale it almost looks unreal. The majority of it is gray, a shade of gray so light you probably wouldn't be able to tell the difference if you put the color white next to it. There are also spots where a shade of blue equally as subtle shows through the gray, but it isn't so easy to see unless you look close enough.

The clouds are big and heavy, and they are floating relatively low in the sky. However, they are much darker than the gray of the sky, which makes them stand out in a way. It's almost as if they're black against a white background; that's how obvious the contrast is.

And lastly, there's the rain. It falls heavily from the muted gray clouds, soaking everyone standing below them in blankets of cold water. When the raindrops touch your skin, the effect is sharp and almost painful. It feels like you're being hit with thousands of tiny needles.

My name is Grace Letterman. I am thirteen years old, about to turn fourteen. In fact, my birthday is tomorrow, on the nineteenth of August. It's quite weird really, that it's raining this much in August, much less raining at all, especially when the weather is supposed to be warm.

Since our family doesn't have much money, I probably won't do anything too special for my birthday. My mother will most likely bake a small cake for me, like she does every year, she and my father will sing Happy Birthday, I will blow out the candles as I make a wish, and that would be my fourteenth birthday.

Even though it's not much to look forward to, we still have a good time together as we celebrate.

I live in a small town in southern California. Our house is at the top of a narrow, curved street, where there are not many other people living around us. The only good thing about where we live is that we're in walking distance of the ocean and the beach, and I like it because I love being near the water. The sound of the waves is comforting, and whenever I need some time alone, I usually visit the beach to take a peaceful walk. It always calms me down, no matter what mood I'm in.

The house we live in is quite small, but it's not like I've ever wished for a better house. It is, indeed, a two story house, but both stories aren't as large as most people would be comfortable with. I've lived in the house all my life, and tomorrow would make it exactly fourteen years in the same small wooden building. All my memories are buried deep within the walls of the house, and it's one reason why I never want to leave. I may not live in paradise, but at least I'm lucky enough to have a place to live, and especially one that I love.

A little over two months ago, my mother was diagnosed with cancer. The hospital is about an hour or so away from where we live, and it is not a very good one either. But it's really all we can get. At the time, my father was forced to rush home from Alabama, where he was currently working for his job. When the doctor told my father and I that she was sick, we were worried, of course, but she'd assured us that it wasn't a severe type of cancer. We were told that she was going to be fine.

I am happy to see that my mother is still up and well. My father's been home with my mother and I for almost two months now, ever since he'd had to come back. I'm happy he's back, but coming back for something like this had cost him his job. He's been trying to find a new place to work, but where I live, searching for a job isn't exactly so easy.

I am trudging through the wet sand on the beach in the rain at five-thirty on a cold Friday evening. I am not sure why the weather changed so suddenly, especially since no one saw it coming. The rain has made the sand turn cold and squishy. Each time I walk, my steps leave footprints in the sand, but they are soon filled up by the rain. When I look behind me, all I see is my trail of rain-filled shoe prints.

The storm had started no more than thirty minutes ago. I was taking a quiet walk on the beach like I normally do when I felt the first few drops of rain. Since it wasn't enough to make me turn back to go home, I thought it was only going to last a few minutes and so I kept going. That's when I felt the wind. And after that, with each minute that passed by, I could slowly feel the raindrops coming down faster and stronger as I walked, and then I'd decided to turn around. Now it had come to this, a full on downpour, and I am still not home yet.

I also feel bad that the rain has ruined my favorite pair of shoes. Before the storm started, I was wearing my only slightly dirty tennis shoes that my father had bought me for my twelfth birthday. Luckily, I had never grown out of them, which is why I still wear them almost every day. But now there is mud and wet sand all over them, and there are holes in the bottom that have formed from the hard pebbles I've been walking on. It's uncomfortable to walk, almost painful to be honest, for the holes in my shoes let the water and sand in, proceeding to soak my socks as well.

I look up into the gushing rain, trying to see my house from here. I can see a little farther into the storm, but there is too much rain to see any further than that. I can barely keep my eyes open with how much wind and water there is. I have a feeling I'm almost there, so I try to walk faster.

I reach the steps at the edge of the shore. The stairs are surrounded by large rocks, and the rocks act as a wall. The stairs are sandy and wet, and I have to be careful while going up so as to not slip on them.

My wet hair sticks to the sides of my face as I keep walking, and the wind only makes everything worse. It wasn't too cold before the storm started, but the weather had completely changed when the cold rain and the fierce wind kicked in.

I walk up the steps to the edge of the road, and I realize

crossing the street with the pouring rain in my way is going to be hard. I shake my head and walk slowly toward the street that I can barely see.

Luckily, there are almost no cars on the road at the moment, and after I watch the last car speedily pass by, I get the sense there won't be any more for the time being and step off the sidewalk into the wet, glistening street.

I kick small pebbles into puddles and hear more of them crunch under my feet as I slowly and carefully make my way across the street. Before I know it, I hear the sound of an engine spurring and move my head to the side in a quick, speedy motion, a burst of fear exploding in my chest.

A shiny black car with watery streaks on the side from the rain running down it squeaks to a stop, and a man with a long beard pokes his head out the window and scowls at me.

"Hey!" he yells loudly in my direction. I see the rainwater spew out of his mouth as he spits the words at me. "Get out of the way before I run you over!"

I hold my hands up innocently in the rain and turn my focus back to the road before I run to the sidewalk waiting for me on the other side. I hear the man in the car swear loudly as I hurry to safety. He then hits the gas pedal with great force and the car speeds away down the street. The tires kick up a spray of water into the air, but luckily I'm far enough away that it doesn't hit me.

I walk along the sidewalk until the end of it comes into view. I turn the corner onto a steep, narrow street; my house is all the way at the top, and I have to climb up a wet, slippery sidewalk to get to it, knowing I could fall at any moment if I'm not careful enough. To make it worse, I would be walking against the wind, so even the strong breeze could throw me off balance. And of course there's still the rain to block my vision, which also adds to my building nervousness.

Finally, after I've steeled up all the hope and courage I have in me, I take a deep breath and start up the steep sidewalk, hoping my worn out shoes still have just enough friction to keep me from losing my footing.

Thankfully, after an incredibly slow and careful climb up the sidewalk, I make it up to my house and walk up to the door. Before I walk inside I lean over with my hands on my knees for a second, taking deep breaths. Getting up here is always hard for me, for I'm not particularly athletic, but in the rain it's almost impossible, especially with my close-to-useless shoes. The hole in the bottom of my right shoe feels like it's gotten bigger, so it's like I'm walking around in just my socks, which is even more uncomfortable, mainly because everywhere I walk, the ground is soaked with water.

I take off my shoes and socks outside and open the door. It makes a creaking sound as it opens, and I walk inside when there's just enough room for me to get in. I stand on the doormat for a few minutes, still dripping wet with water.

I realize how cold I really am when the door closes again and there's suddenly no fierce wind blowing my way. I stand shivering uncontrollably on the mat, the water trickling off my hair onto it, and my clothes clinging to me in an awkward way due to how much water they'd absorbed.

I twist my hair in my hands and squeeze all the water out of it onto the mat. I'm shivering a little less violently now and once almost all the water has dripped out of my clothes, I decide I'm decent enough to walk at this point.

I head over in the direction of the kitchen, where my mother will most likely be waiting for me. Our kitchen isn't large; to be honest, it's more on the small and cramped side. It mainly consists of a tiny metal sink, a stove, a refrigerator with a few magnets and things on it that have been there for many years now, a couple cupboards on the back wall, one below the sink, and the smallest pantry you could imagine, barely big enough to fit everything we need inside of it. Other than that, there's a dinner table on the far side of the kitchen, a ceiling light above it, and that's about it.

Sure enough, I see my mother at the table, reading a book. She seems fully engrossed in the novel, and she's reading with wide eyes. She hears me as I walk in though, and she looks up at me.

"My goodness!" she exclaims rather loudly when she notices what a bad state I'm in. "You're soaking wet! The storm has really been that bad?"

I nod my head, my bangs spraying small drops of water over my face. I rub my eyes as I reply, "I bet it's one of the worst storms we've had in a while."

My mother frowns and clicks her tongue. "It's not good for you to be out in the rain like this. Go upstairs and take a warm shower - you'll feel better."

I nod again. "Thanks, Mom," I say as I turn for the stairs. We have a narrow staircase, and the stairs themselves are hard, brown wood, easy to slip on if you hurry up too fast. It's even easier to trip if you're wet, like me. They're also spaced rather far apart, so you have to stretch your legs to get to the next one as you go up.

I get in the shower, and the warm water feels good on my freezing body as it melts away the coldness in seconds. When I'm finished, I put on a fresh pair of dry clothes and smile to myself. I feel amazing.

Grabbing my wet clothes from the bathroom floor, I walk into the closet in my room and throw them carelessly into the laundry hamper on top of the rest of my dirty clothes. I realize I haven't done my laundry in a while, so I make a mental note to do it soon.

I rush back down the stairs to meet my mother in the kitchen again. She's still reading her book; it makes me happy to see how relaxed and peaceful she is.

When she notices my improved condition, she smiles one of her warm, kind smiles. "How do you feel?" she asks.

"Great," I admit. "Like a new person."

"Good." Her smile gets wider.

Everyone who's seen me smile says I have my mother's smile, which is true. I do look remarkably like her rather than my father; the only thing I get from him is his eyes. Those dark, solemn gray eyes that everyone finds striking even though I think they give off more of a subtle appearance. But eye color is a good feature to have, as I've learned to accept over time. It's the one feature you can't be insecure about, the one feature that fits everyone, no matter who you are. Everything else about us is adjustable, our style, our personality, our clothing. But eye color is the one thing we can't change. Everyone's individual eye color is unique. It's made to fit them, and no one else.

"Why don't you make yourself something to eat?" my mother suggests. "If you're up for a sandwich, everything's in the fridge. Help yourself."

"Thanks," I say again with another smile. I am incredibly hungry, to tell the truth, especially after that long walk through the storm.

Opening the fridge, I find it's easy to spot the bread, cheese, turkey, and lettuce. The tomatoes, however, are hidden beneath various fruits and vegetables in one of the drawers, and I have to fish around to finally find them. After I have all the ingredients, I head to the counter and begin assembling my sandwich.

This process doesn't take me long to do. I'm done making the sandwich in less than five minutes, and I turn to one of the cupboards on the back wall to get a plate. Once I've put my food on it, I settle in at the table in the chair next to my mother and start eating.

I devour the sandwich quickly, almost in the amount of time it took me to make it. I lean back in my chair, plate empty, finally satisfied.

"Where's Dad?" I ask when it comes to my attention that I haven't seen him since I got home.

"Oh, your father went to the market to get some things," my mother answers. "I'm sure he'll be back soon."

"Oh." I pick up my plate to put it in the sink, and then I hear the sound of the front door opening. That must be my father, and I run over to see if I'm right, happy to find that I am.

He is still outside, luckily out of the rain though. I notice that he's carrying two brown paper bags, both of which I assume are filled with things from the market he'd supposedly just come back from. Seeing he's having some trouble carrying both of them at the same time, I rush over to help.

I take one of the bags from him as he willingly hands it over to me. It weighs more than I expect, and I find I have to use both my hands to carry it the right way.

My father and I take the two bags into the house and set them down beside the coat rack. After putting them down, I straighten up and turn toward my father, who is taking off his coat to put on the rack.

"You're not wet," I observe out loud, frowning. "How did you stay dry out there?"

My father simply shrugs his shoulders as he looks down to inspect himself. "Believe it or not, it stopped raining for a while and luckily just at the right time. I managed to get back before it started coming down nearly as hard again."

I nod when he's done explaining. "It's good you got lucky," I tell him. "No wonder you aren't soaking wet."

"It hadn't completely stopped though," he says. "It was a little more than a sprinkle, but it wasn't pouring like it was before. And believe me, it isn't easy to carry heavy bags of food in the rain."

I smile. "How hard was that?"

He returns my smile. "It wasn't the easiest," he replies, holding his arms out to give me a hug.

I laugh softly as I hug him. Suddenly, I hear a sound on the roof; perhaps something had hit it. I immediately run to the closest window and open the blinds to peer outside into the rain.

Like I'd assumed, I see small pieces of icy hail falling from the sky. The tiny pieces hit the ground and roof above with light thudding noises, along with the rest of the unfrozen drops of water. I like hearing the sound of the raindrops though, especially now that it isn't raining as hard as it was before. In fact, I think I could fall asleep listening to it. It's peaceful, the sound of the rain.

My father joins me at my side in front of the window, listening to the rain as well. We're both quiet for a minute, concentrating on the sound, until I break the silence.

"Do you ever wonder what life would be like if it was always peaceful, like the sound of the rain?" I ask him.

He seems surprised by the question. I almost never ask questions like this, though I usually think about them inside my head. He slowly nods, and I continue.

"It would be so nice." I shift my gaze back to the scene of the falling rain as I speak. "Nothing to worry about, no problems... our life would always be like the comforting sounds of light raindrops."

My father places a hand on my shoulder, but I don't look at him.

"She's going to be okay," I hear him say to me. I don't turn my head yet; I am still watching the rain fall softly outside the window.

"But imagine our life if it was like that," I insist. "It would be so... perfect. And you would have a good job, and Mom would still be able to do everything... and we'd have more money and-"

"Stop," my father tells me firmly. I finally turn to look him in the eyes, and his expression is serious as he lowers his voice when he speaks again. "She *will* be okay."

"You don't know that," I immediately counter. "The doctor said nothing would happen, but that could change. They could be wrong... about everything. And what would we do then? What-"

My father's hand slips off my shoulder and I hear him get up. He walks away from the window, and disappears into the kitchen. I sigh and turn back to the rain.

• • •

I open my eyes. My vision is blurry at first, but in a few seconds it clears up and I realize I'm still staring at the window, though from far away now. I think I'd fallen asleep. It's another few seconds before I remember *how* exactly that had happened.

I was still watching the rain from the couch, where I'd laid down what felt like about an hour ago. I guess I'd drifted off there, lying on the comfortable cushions. It's dark now, though, so I can't see the rain falling anymore. I can see the drops rolling down the glass of the window, however, and they leave thin streaks of water behind them when they do. I can still hear it too, the soft pitter-patter noises on the roof. And I can tell from the sound of it that it's still falling softly outside, probably in a light drizzle, just like before I'd fallen asleep. It tells me that the worst part of the storm has probably passed, and now it's presumably coming to an end.

I sit up and rub my eyes. As soon as I've relieved the rest of the sleep from them, I walk over to the window a few feet away and close the blinds after watching the small drops of water roll down the glass one more time. I turn around to find that a fragrant smell is drifting my way, and it smells so good it makes my mouth water.

I start toward the kitchen, and I enter to see my father at the table, reading the newspaper, and my mother at the counter near the stove, making food for dinner. I advance toward her, and then I'm at her side, watching her cut long carrots into thin slices.

She notices me and glances my way, but only for a second before she turns back to the carrots. "Have you gotten some rest?" she asks me.

I suddenly remember when I'd told my father about the sound of the rain, and how it compares to life. I don't really know why I'd said it, and I don't quite remember what was really going through my mind at the time. I try not to think about it too much for the moment.

I nod in response to my mother's question as the thought finally disappears to the back of my mind for the time being. "I'm glad I fell asleep. I was exhausted."

"I would agree. Anyone would be weary after doing what you did today."

"Yeah, I guess I have some courage in me to walk back from that far in the rain," I say jokingly, a smile cracking on my lips. I remember the man who'd almost hit me with his shiny black car, but I don't tell my mother about it, since she already has enough on her mind. I don't need to worry her any further.

"What's for dinner?" I ask instead, changing the subject.

"Chicken and roasted carrots," she answers as she sets the carrot slices aside. She then takes one of the two other carrots sitting beside the cutting board and begins slicing it as she continues. "Are you hungry?"

I wasn't before, but I am now, especially since the smell of the chicken cooking in the oven is the only thing I'm thinking about now. "Yes, I am," I reply.

"Well, you're in luck," my mother tells me. "The chicken's almost ready, and these carrots won't take long to make. Maybe just a little longer."

I nod my head again. To be honest, I don't mind how long it takes, I just can't wait to eat it. My mother's cooking is the best food on this planet. When she makes food, it doesn't matter what she cooks, you just know it's going to be amazing. It's the kind of food where the flavor continues to linger in your mouth after you've eaten it, and the taste is so unique and unlike anything else you've tasted. My father cooks incredibly well too - he's learned a lot from my mother - and I always consider myself so lucky that my parents can cook amazing food for me whenever I want it. Not many people have that.

My mother only cooks on rare occasions, and today she must be making food because it's the day before my birthday. I always get excited when she cooks for us, and I know that even though she doesn't make her special recipes often, it's a good thing because I enjoy them more when she surprises us.

I remember when I was younger, I used to always have a dream of my parents opening a restaurant, because with their cooking there's no doubt the place would be busy every minute of the day. But with what's recently happened, I know that probably won't work out until my mother hopefully gets better. I'm not completely letting go of that dream though. I'm planning to still hold onto it for the small chance that it might work out in the future.

It's only a couple more minutes before my mother sets down a plate of delightful chicken, rice, and roasted carrots in front of me and my father at the table. There's surprisingly enough for all three of us to eat as much as we want, and even then there would probably be leftovers. My stomach makes a rumbling noise again as I feel the hunger once more.

My mother cuts each of us a piece of chicken and puts the separate pieces in each of our plates. I ask for extra carrots since there's quite a large amount of those as well, and my mother uses a big spoon to scoop them up and put them in my plate next to the chicken and rice. When I think I have enough food to fill my stomach, I thank her and dig in.

I'm so hungry it's hard to keep from eating too much at a time. The food tastes delicious. After I eat the last bite of chicken and rice from my plate, my stomach is full again, and I'm happy to know that I don't need any more food.

"How was it?" asks my mother.

"It was amazing," I tell her. "It's the best I've eaten in a long time."

"Good." She smiles.

I glance up at the small, worn out clock hanging high on the wall next to me that we've had there ever since I can remember. It reads eight-forty six. I had no idea it was this late! We don't usually eat dinner at this time of the night, but my parents must have waited for me since I'd fallen asleep a little while earlier. After all, I had come home from the beach a little later than I'd hoped to because of the storm, but at least I'd gotten to eat a great dinner.

I wait for my parents to finish eating, nonetheless, and then I give them each a hug before going upstairs. Since I'm not as tired as I would've wanted to be, I decide to read. I have a strong passion for reading, and I read more than I do a lot of other things. I enjoy it; in fact, I could read my whole life if I chose to do nothing else. It's one of those things that you can never get tired of, something you could sit down and do all day if you wanted to. That's why I like it so much.

My room is small, much like all the other rooms and the house itself. But I try to fit in as much as I possibly can. My bed, for instance, takes up most of the space, pushed up all the way against the left wall. On top of it rests a handmade quilt, a quilt I made myself after my mother taught me how to sew a few years ago when I was a little younger. I am very proud of the quilt, for it's the best thing I've made since I've learned to sew.

My book sits on top of the quilt that I'd folded up this morning after I'd woken up and gotten out of bed. I'd started reading *Little Women* a few days ago, and I'm already more than halfway through it. I've always been an advanced reader, but that only means I have a larger selection of books to choose from. I quite like that I have that advantage, for not many people my age do.

I climb up onto my bed after unfolding the quilt and grab my book. I open it to the page I'd left off on and, as soon as I begin, I get lost in the story and forget about everything else as I read.

I can definitely say that time goes by quickly when you're reading, especially if you're like me and it's hard to close the book once you've started. When I can finally tear my eyes away from the book to look at the time, I am quite surprised when I see that it's nearing ten-thirty.

Realizing that I'm actually more exhausted than I'd assumed I would be at this time, I decide to close the book and try to sleep. After I mark my page, I lean over to put the book on the bedside table and turn the lamp off. The room instantly gets dark and everything around me turns to black. I can't see anything for a few minutes, but once my eyes adjust to the darkness a little more, I can barely make out the shape of the door only a small distance away and the tiny table next to me. I finally get under the covers and pull the quilt up to my chin as I close my eyes.

I am fast asleep until the sirens outside my window suddenly wake me up.

●  ●  ●

I open my eyes to the loud, frightening sound. When the sirens don't stop, I sit bolt upright in bed. I look at my window, which I assume one of my parents must have opened to let some cool air in, since my room is always warmer than the others. I also notice a red light coming from the open window, illuminating the white wall.

I pull the quilt off and hurry to the window to see what's going on. The wind whisks in my face, making me squint, but I can still see clearly enough.

There are three red trucks waiting outside our house. The bright red lights on the top are flashing incessantly. I recognize them. *Ambulances*.

Could they be here because…

*No*. I cannot bring myself to think the next few words that I'm desperately hoping aren't true. My mother was fine. She had to be.

I turn away from the window and run for the door of my room. I scramble down the stairs and head straight for my parents' bedroom. I barely notice that the front door is open, sending cool wind throughout the house.

The door to my mother's bedroom is open, and I can hear my heart beating loudly in my chest, despite the loud wind and continuous sirens still going on outside. My father is standing in the room, along with a few other men. I direct my gaze to the bed in the center of the room. My mother is still sleeping.

I calm down a bit, but my father doesn't seem to calm down at all. He appears to be speaking loudly to the men beside him, but the wind and sirens drown out most of his voice.

I walk over to him. "What's going on?" I ask impatiently, my voice edged with doubt and fear.

My father looks down at me. "Oh, Grace.." he says, his voice trailing off, leaving the sentence unfinished. He doesn't need to continue for me to know what he was going to say.

I remember again what I said to my father yesterday by the window while watching the rain fall from the clouds. *The doctors could be wrong.* That's the only sentence I can remember. I can't believe I could ever say something like that. How could I be that thoughtless?

Maybe I just didn't know what I was doing. I don't know, but I can't think about it anymore. The tears well up in my eyes, but I don't let them spill over yet.

"No," I say firmly. "She can't be gone. She can't be!"

I rush over to her side and take her hand, which is by her face on the pillow. I put it to my own face, and remember everything about her that I loved.

The sirens have finally stopped blaring outside. Refusing to believe my mother was really gone, just like that in the middle of the night, I lean down and put my ear to her heart. I can't hear anything, but I convince myself that it must be because of the loud wind.

I sit back up and put my other hand on her heart instead. My hope and fear diminishes, replaced by dread and sadness. I can't feel a thing.

My mother's hand is still on my cheek. I keep it there as I lean back on my heels and let the tears come. I can't forgive myself for what I said.

And I know I never will either.

17

*Chapter 2:*

*Shocked*

I am fourteen years old, and I have been for over a week now. I still don't know why the worst thing that had ever happened to me had to occur on my fourteenth birthday. And I'm afraid I will never know why.

That day had gone by in a blur, but somehow I still remember everything that had happened quite distinctly. I don't like that I remember everything so well, because of all the days I recall fairly clearly, that one is with no doubt the worst.

It hurts to remember though, and I can't think about it without tears welling up in my eyes and blurring my vision. But it's hard to forget someone who's been so important in your life. Someone who's been with you every moment you can remember. It's hard to forget how you sat next to them with their hand pressed tight against your cheek, crying. It's one of those things that will be with you for your entire life, until the day you die.

It is September first, almost two weeks after my birthday and the tragic morning I experienced. I'm sure that I can relate to anyone else in the world that has gone through what I had. I can't imagine anything worse than the day my mother died.

And I'm absolutely sure of it.

• • •

I open my eyes to a warm and sunny morning. When I am completely awake and I can think clearly, I realize that this is the first time I had no frightening dreams in my sleep. I slept soundly the entire night, which is new and a relief to me.

Since the sun is already high in the sky, I feel like it's a little later in the morning than I would have wanted to get up. But it doesn't matter; it's not like I have anything important planned for today. I never do anymore.

I stand up and begin to fold my quilt so it's not a mess on the top of my bed. Sometimes things bother me when they're messy; I know for a fact that I'd gotten that from my mother. I try to keep everything around me as clean as possible, but there are of course those few times when I'm not as careful.

Once my quilt is folded into a perfect square and I've put it near the end of my bed, I straighten and flatten down my sheets and head to my closet to change into a fresh pair of clothes for the day.

For the past couple days I've been taking walks on the beach in the morning right after I wake up, just because I like the way the breeze feels early in the morning. Besides, walks on the beach are relaxing, and sometimes I need to be relaxed to let go of everything for a while. Walking usually helps me get my mind off things most of the time, and I can listen to the peaceful chirping of the birds as I stroll along the shore, the cool water running over my feet, my toes digging into the soft sand.

I change into a decent pair of jeans (not my favorite pair, but it will do for something as simple as a walk on the beach), and short-sleeved white shirt with handpainted flowers on the front. This is one of my favorite shirts - it's the one my grandmother bought for me as a Christmas present last year. I only put it on once in awhile since it's so special to me, and plus I don't want to make it worn out too soon.

I make sure to get hold of my sweater as well, which is lying on my bedpost. I remember I'd put it there a few days ago when I'd worn it just so it'd be easier to find and I wouldn't have to search the house for it afterwards. I want to take it just in case it's chillier outside than I'm expecting. I don't want to wear it now though, so I simply tie it around my waist for the time being.

The last thing I do is get ready to fix my hair; I just comb through it as quickly as I can without paying much attention to it and let it be free instead of spending time braiding it again. Since it's a little late in the morning, I need to hurry before it gets too hot outside.

I'm not exactly hungry, but if I'm going to be gone for a while, I'm assuming it'd be good to eat something before I go. I decide on eating something that won't take long to consume, so I choose a simple bowl of oatmeal.

I grab a box of it from our pantry and fish out a medium-sized packet. I take the carton of milk from our refrigerator and pour everything in a small bowl. Since it is already pre-made with all the flavoring and sugar, I only have to add the milk and warm it up for about a minute in the microwave.

I sit down at the table and start eating. When I finish about half of what's in the bowl, I start to wonder where my father is. He isn't here with me in the kitchen where he usually is in the morning reading a newspaper or something of that sort, so maybe he is still sleeping. He already knows that I leave the house every morning to go for a walk on the beach, so I don't have to tell him before I go.

After I'm done eating and I've used my spoon to get every last bit of oatmeal and milk from the bowl, I head over to the sink where I wash the bowl. When I'm done I walk out of the kitchen and toward the door, where I slide on my old pair of shoes. I don't wear them that often, but since my new pair is ruined, I don't really mind wearing these.

I leave the house and start walking down the steep sidewalk to get back to the road below where the cars and people are. The air is still a little chilly, even despite the sun, which is blinding my vision as I walk. But the weather is comfortable - if there was no wind it would be too hot, so I'm glad there's a slight breeze. I cross the street, being alert and careful in case an unexpected car appears.

I walk down the sandy steps before I walk toward the shore, where the water is washing over the small pebbles and the sand is a slightly darker color where the waves have been rolling over it. I like to walk near there because the water at this beach is never freezing; it's just the right temperature so it's comfortable to walk in when the sun is hot on my back.

I can't help thinking about my mother again. I wonder why she had to disappear from my life. Just like that. It wasn't fair. My mother and I just had this connection that was unique and powerful, different from even my father and my best friend Sarah. When I needed someone to talk to, she was the first person I'd go to. I used to tell her everything, regardless of whether it was something that was bothering me or just telling her about my day. Seeing her peacefully in her bed with her eyes closed for the last time was something I could never forget.

The past few days I've been able to let everything on the beach take my focus away from my mother, but today is one of those days that the thought of her just manages to crawl its way back into my head, and it takes a while before I can finally put my attention on something else. Besides, today it's unusually quiet, which is odd. Today is Friday, a day when the streets are supposed to be busy with people rushing to get to work. I decide that maybe it was busier earlier in the morning before I woke up, since I awoke later than usual.

I continue walking calmly along the shore. The water comes up even higher this time, all the way up to my shins. I roll up my jeans some more, just so the edges don't get soaked with water. I watch as more pieces of seaweed get washed onto the shore, pieces that are even bigger than the ones that came before them. I like looking at the seaweed, because even though each piece is the same, the intricate patterns are slightly different. I don't quite know why observing this kind of things is interesting to me, but I'm one of those people that find even simple things fascinating.

I am nearing the end of my walk- I see the giant wall of rocks before me, even though they are still a reasonable distance away. There is more sand here, but there is also a narrower space between where the waves wash onto the shore and the rock wall that has been stretching on to the right of me ever since I've started walking. The wall is shaped like a half-circle that curves around as you walk, which is why the edges of the half-circle are where the beach ends and where I eventually have to stop walking.

I am even closer to the end now and I can see even smaller waves crashing into the rocks at the bottom of the wall, water spraying everywhere as they come into contact with them. It makes a loud sound when it hits, and all the sounds of the beach come together in that moment, like music. It's exactly like music actually, because when you're listening to music, you notice how the beat and the rhythm and the melody and the harmony instantly come together to create a catchy tune, and that's exactly what the sounds on the beach portray when you're listening to them. It's yet another one of my interesting discoveries.

As I'm getting even closer to the wall, a sudden wave crashes into a jagged rock, sending the water up in a violent spray, showering me with small drops of it. I smile to myself and squeeze my eyes shut from the unexpected spray, and when I open them again, I look up to find myself standing in front of the ten-foot high wall of rocks.

I don't usually decide to do things like this, but today feels like a perfect day to take this type of risk. Carefully, after scanning the wall one last time, I begin climbing up, using the jagged pieces and parts in between where a new rock is stacked onto the one below it as footholds to get to the top.

I've always had a natural talent for rock climbing, so it doesn't take much time or effort to get to the top. I use my hands and knees to pull myself up onto the highest rock - which, thankfully, has a flatter surface than the rest of the rocks, so it will be easier to stand on.

I am still crouching on the rock, and now I stand up straight. I am very high up off the ground, higher than I'd expected myself to be when I was looking up at this point from below. I cannot be vulnerable to the water that sprays when it hits the rocks at the bottom now, and I am thankful for that. Because now, even though I don't have the water to cool me down, I have the wind instead.

The cool air blows my hair behind my head, which makes it easier to observe my surroundings since strands of it aren't blocking my vision anymore. I can look at everything from a much higher elevation now, and I like it better than looking at it from down below because there's much more to see from up here.

Behind me, I see a narrow cement pathway winding on for several meters, and since it's so long I can't follow it with my eyes to see the end of it. Beside the pathway on the right are multiple grass fields; each field is separated by sidewalk that runs in between them, and I can see the grass being gently swayed from side to side by the wind. It's a pleasant sight, and it looks so interesting to watch from up here.

In front of me is the ocean, the beautiful blue-green ocean that stretches on for several miles across the earth. The waves that are farther away seem small and harmless, but I know that if I were closer it would look different. I can hear those waves though, despite the fact that I'm up here and they are so far away.

To the right of me is another row of grass fields, again separated by the sidewalks in between them, and the long pathway is still running along the middle of it all. The beach doesn't continue after this point of course, because these rocks are where it ends. But everything is such a beautiful sight, and I wish I could stay up here longer so I can keep watching the people walk on the pathways down below and listen to the waves.

But I know I've been here for too long already. My father must be wondering why I'm still gone, for since I woke up later than either of us usually expects me to, I would have been home quite a while ago.

I sigh and look down, managing to notice a barely visible place between two large rocks that could easily act as the perfect foothold. And it's a little farther than halfway down this wall, which will make my climb back to the ground a little easier once I get to that point.

I sit down on the edge with my legs hanging off the side, and place one of my feet on a smaller foothold I also manage to catch a glimpse of. After that I continue to find places to put my feet like I did climbing up until I reach the bigger, safer foothold I'd noticed earlier.

When I feel I'm close enough to the ground that it isn't necessary to climb down the rest of the wall, I loosen my grip on the rocks I'm holding on to with my hands and drop safely to the ground.

The time it takes to walk back home from the beach is less than I expected. Either that or I'm just so lost in my own thoughts that I don't notice how fast my house comes into view.

I meet my father in the living room. He is sitting on the couch, reading another newspaper, like I always expect him to be. I sit down beside him, and he looks up at me when he hears me walk up.

"How was your walk?" he asks me. "It was a little chilly today, wasn't it?"

I nod. "A little, but was refreshing," I tell him. "I watched the waves from the top of a rock."

"You climbed that wall again?" he asks, smiling, his tone edged with surprise.

I nod again. "Yes. But don't worry. I'm good at climbing walls remember? I used to do it all the time when I was little."

And it's true. When I was younger, my parents always used to take me to the nearby fairs in the park. We would always find the rock climbing wall in the middle of all the madness, and it would be my favorite thing to do, besides eating all the sugary sweets and desserts my small stomach could possibly hold. I don't realize I'm smiling as I think about those old times.

My father notices though. "Thinking about those fairs, huh?" he wonders aloud with a smile like the one still planted on my face. I don't know how, but my father's always had a talent for reading my mind and knowing what I'm thinking all the time. Sometimes it's a good thing.

I know he already knows the answer to that question, but I say it anyway. "Yes," I admit. "I miss when we used to do things like that."

My father nods. "I do too. But we can do that again, can't we? Even though you're older, I'm sure you'll still enjoy all those activities."

I look down at my hands for a moment. "But… it won't be the same," I insist. "Without… Mom." I hesitate between the words. I'm still looking down.

"We can still have fun though, right?" my father persists. "Even without her." He doesn't hesitate like I did, but I can still hear the sadness tinting his words.

I don't look up, and he continues.

"Why don't we go tomorrow?" he suggests. "I heard there's a fair in the park close by. And tomorrow's Saturday. We'll be there nine o'clock sharp."

I consider it. It does sound fun, and I have to admit that I do miss spending time with father. After all, I've barely spent any time with him after my mother died, besides the funeral and a couple times during the day.

I finally look up to meet his gaze. "All right," I agree.

He smiles happily.

*Chapter 3:*

*Picking Myself Up*

I watch from the window of the taxi as the outside world passes by in a blur. The trees and cars and houses and buildings and people all seem blended together in a mix of different colors and shapes as we drive by them, but it looks interesting in a way, too. Each time we stop at a traffic light, everything suddenly stops moving, except for the people of course. Then when we start driving again, the world goes back to a blur.

The red light in front of us turns green and the taxi driver hits the gas pedal, jerking us back into motion. My head snaps back slightly from the sudden movement, and this isn't the first time the driver's done something this sudden. I hate that we always have to travel around by taxi, because it's clear that most of the drivers aren't careful ones. They drive around like there's no danger in going faster than expected, or making sudden turns that make the passengers jump around in their seats. I hear my father mutter something under his breath in the seat in front of me; I hope the driver didn't hear him.

I am sitting in the back of the car. The driver is in the seat one row ahead in front of the wheel, and my father is next to him in the passenger's seat. The floor of the vehicle is a bit too dirty for my liking, food wrappers and paper and garbage scattered all over it. Everything makes me wonder when this car was last cleaned, and it doesn't seem like recently from what I've noticed.

The smell isn't the most pleasant either. I can't exactly describe what it's like inside the car, but it's definitely not something people would call fresh. It smells more old than new, but more than that there's a sort of chemical smell as well, and it makes me want to gag every time I inhale a breath of air. I try not to focus on it too much, and to help I open the window next to me, which lets in fresh air so I'm not as miserable.

The driver makes a speedy turn around the corner of a long street and the car swerves to the right, making us move with it. I jerk to the side, my head snapping to the right. I'm glad the window is open, because if it wasn't I would've hit my head on it, hard. I curse under my breath and gather myself as we begin driving straight again.

My annoyance level has escalated even more now, but I know I can't do anything about how carelessly the driver is driving. And neither can my father. If we do, he'll obviously make my father pay more for complaining, and we only have enough on us for the drive to the park and back, plus a little more for lunch and to pay for our tickets to get into the fair. We always keep a little extra on us as well, but I don't want my father to have to use it to pay a taxi driver more money for complaining about his reckless driving. As hard as it is, I will have to keep quiet.

The driver makes another turn, and it still makes me sway to the side a bit, but it isn't as bad as the last one. Thankfully, after this turn we pull up next to the sidewalk near the park and the driver hits the brake. My father thanks him and pays him a fair amount of money for the distance we traveled, and then we get out of the car. After I close my door and it slams back into place, the tires squeal and the taxi disappears down the street.

It's a fairly warm day. The sun is hot on my back, but the soft breeze makes it cooler than it would be if there wasn't any. My father and I wait until there is a pause between the rushing cars and then we quickly cross the street to the other side.

We wait for a minute as I take the time to notice each and every little thing about the fair. The park is huge; I did not expect that so much would be able to fit here. It looks like we arrived at just the right time because it seems that the people running the events have just finished setting up the tents where they will take place. There are three long rows of tents in front of us where all the games will be, and even though there are a lot of them, they're small games so my father and I can try to do as many as we can. That is, if the lines aren't too long, which I'm assuming they probably won't be, considering the fact that we got here early.

Behind all the tents is an even more breathtaking sight. That's where all the rides are, all the big, tall, exciting rides. The ferris wheel is the one that instantly catches my attention, since that's the biggest ride I see among all of them. I'm pretty sure that will also be the most amazing one, especially if we do it at night. I also manage to spot the rock climbing wall, which is across from the ferris wheel next to another really enjoyable-looking ride. I'm definitely planning on doing that one as well.

"Ah," my father says, pointing somewhere not too far off in the distance. "I believe that's where we register."

I follow his finger in the direction he's pointing until I see exactly what he's looking at. He's pointing to a tent at the far left of the grass field, closer to where the field ends and the last of the tents for the actual events end. As I look closer, I see that the tent he's pointing at is slightly bigger than the others and I immediately realize it's the registration tent. You have to register to get into the actual fair, and you can get your tickets there too if you don't have them yet. Luckily, we have ours already, but we have to register anyway.

We begin walking in the direction of the registration tent and, as we get closer, I am happy to see that the line isn't that long yet, and I realize that perhaps it's because we arrived earlier than most people do. Of course, the fair is an all-day event, so people can come and go whenever they want. I suspect we might have to stay all day, but it'll be fun, so it's not like we'll have to leave.

I move to the side a bit so I can see the registration desk. There is a woman at the front who is giving people their tickets, and she looks quite friendly to me. She is wearing a red collared shirt with a name tag displaying her name, Amanda, on the front. I watch as a young couple leaves the desk holding their tickets and laughing together. I smile as I see how happy they are; and I know even more now that this will be one of the most enjoyable days I've had in a long time.

I get back in line next to my father and notice a family of three standing in line in front of us: two parents and a little girl of maybe about six or seven. She seems so happy, laughing and grinning wildly. She is carrying a large teddy bear under her right arm, and she's tugging on her mother's hand and pointing off into the distance at one of the tents. I watch as her mother looks down at her and smiles.

I do the same, except I'm only smiling to myself. I can't help seeing myself in the little girl - she's acting so much like the way I used to when I was her age. It hurts to remember though, so I quickly try to put the thought out of my mind. I already miss my mother so much, and remembering things about her makes me miss her so much more. I continue to watch silently but with the smile still on my face as she bounces up and down on her toes.

The line moves up some more, and a little while after the family in front of us is at the front of the line. The little girl is still bouncing, not able to stay still, and I admire how energetic she is. I find myself wishing I was still like that.

"Hello sir," the woman at the desk says with a smile to the little girl's father. "May I see your tickets, please?"

"We were told we would be able to buy them here," he says, reaching into his pocket.

The woman nods. "Absolutely. That'll be exactly twenty-four dollars for the three of you."

The man pulls some money out of his pockets and counts everything he has. After a few seconds he looks back up and doesn't say anything for a second. "I don't have enough."

The girl turns and buries her face in her mother's shirt. My heart sinks. I hate to see the girl like this. It's worse than thinking about my mother. I feel a desperate need to help the family, but what can I do?

Then my father taps the girl's father on the shoulder. "Is this enough?" he asks, holding out some money. My hopes lift again.

The man turns and looks back and forth from the money to my father. "Yes," he says, relieved. "How will I ever thank you?"

"No need," my father assures him. "I think your daughter deserves to have fun here."

The girl looks up now, face wet with tears. She's now smiling widely again, like when I first saw her earlier. I smile back at her, and I feel alive with happiness again.

"She sure does," the girl's father agrees. Then he looks at me. "After all, they do grow up fast."

I smile. He turns back around and hands the money to the woman at the desk. About a minute later, she hands him back three tickets. "Have a wonderful time," she tells him with a polite smile.

"Thank you so much," he says, then turns around one more time toward us. "And to you too," he tells us.

My father and I nod back at him. The little girl is jumping up and down like she was before as she walks. I'm glad we helped the family, because not only did they remind me so much of my family a few years ago, but they also seemed so excited about this fair that I couldn't stand to see them disappointed.

Besides, what my father said was right. If that little girl's like me, it will be something she remembers for the rest of her life. Experiences like this are things that will always be special to you, no matter who you are.

I watch as the family makes their way to their first tent, and the girl's parents step back as the woman at the tent hands her a small plastic ball. I continue to observe as the girl throws the ball forward. It must be one of those games with the bowls of water and if you manage to throw the ball in one of the bowls, you get a prize. I used to get so excited about games like that, and I even remember how mad I used to get when I didn't win a prize. The memory makes me smile again.

My father gives our tickets to the woman at the desk, and after she looks at them for a second, she hands them back to us and tells to have a good day. My father tells her same, and then we begin walking toward the tents.

"Thank you for helping that family," I say to my father, looking up at him.

He nods. "They deserve to have fun," he tells me. "I couldn't let them leave without getting a chance to explore this place."

"Thank you," I say. "I couldn't stand to see the look on that little girl's face. It reminded me of myself, how I would feel if that was me."

"Well, at least now they'll get to enjoy themselves," my father says with a smile. Then he looks at me. "And so will we."

I nod happily.

Two hours go by as if it's just five minutes. For the past few hours my father and I have been doing every game at each tent one after another. There are so many tents set up and so many different games that we've only gone through about half of them. But that's also because there have been some relatively longer lines for the last few games we've done. Luckily, we hadn't had to stand too long in those lines though, and the games were still worth the wait.

I had begun to get hungry a little while ago, so I'd suggested to my father that we take a quick break to get something to eat. He had agreed, so we had started walking around to find somewhere we could get food. We had found a place with luckily a relatively short line that has the normal food they always sell at fairs and carnivals: burgers, hot dogs, things like that. Which I don't completely mind - even though I don't particularly like food like that, it's better than nothing. And besides, I'm sure it won't be that bad.

We've already ordered our food and now we're just waiting at the counter for it. I'm glad we got in the line when we did, because as I look back now, the line has gotten closer to twice as long as before. Ordering food isn't what holds up the line though, it's waiting for it that takes longer. Finally, the person who took our order comes back with a large brown paper bag filled with our food and hands it to my father.

"Drinks are over there," he tells us, pointing to our right. My father thanks him as we take our food and head that way.

My father looks around to find an empty table as I fill up two medium-sized plastic cups with water and ice for us. He finally spots a table not too far away and points to it. I see that it's mostly in the shade, which is perfect. I carry the two waters and my father carries the food as we start heading toward the table. I feel my stomach makes a strong growling noise - I guess I was hungrier than I thought.

I take my burger out of the paper bag and start eating as soon as we sit down. It's much better than I expected it to be, but that's probably because anything tastes good when you're really hungry. As I take a few sips of my water, I notice that my father seems to be enjoying his food as well.

He looks up at me after taking another bite of his burger. "How do you like your food?" he asks me.

"Not bad," I reply. "It's actually pretty good."

He smiles. "Good. But I bet I can even make a better burger than this," he adds jokingly.

I laugh. "I'm sure you can," I agree.

I finish the last bite of my food and wait for my father to do so as well. We both drink the last few sips of our water and walk over to the trash can nearby to throw the rest of our trash away. Afterwards, my father turns and looks and me.

"What do you want to do next?" he asks me.

I think about it for a second. "Maybe we should finish doing the rest of those games," I suggest. "I want to wait to do the rides until it starts getting darker. That's when they'll be the most fun."

My father nods. "You're right," he agrees. "If the lines for the games haven't gotten too much longer, I'm sure we'll be able to finish the rest of them."

I smile and nod in agreement as we start heading back towards the tents.

The sun has just about started to set. I've started to get a little tired, but definitely not too much to go home yet. After all, we still haven't done any of the rides yet, and I don't want to miss those, especially since we waited all day to do them at night.

I think this fair will be the most fun at night. Everything will be lit up and it will look so amazing. I don't want to stay too late, because I don't think a lot of people will be around then and I'm sure the people running all the events and supervising the rides are going to need everyone to leave at a certain time so they can get ready to go home. But it won't be long from now until it gets dark anyway - after the sun sets, it'll only take about half an hour. So we'll still be able to do plenty of rides at night without staying later than we want to.

"Are you ready to go on the rides?" my father's voice comes from beside me. "I'm sure everyone's going to start heading over there soon since the sun's already started to set."

"You're right," I agree. "We can start doing a few of them now. But I want to save the ferris wheel for last. I think it'll be the best if we do that one once it's completely dark."

My father nods as we start making our way over to the area where all the rides are. There aren't too many people over there now, but like my father said, this area is probably going to get filled up quickly in only a matter of time. So we really better start getting as many rides as we can do before the lines get too long.

I remember the rock climbing wall and look around until I find it not too far away from where we're standing. I point to it and look at my father. "I want to do that first," I tell him. "It's always been one of my favorites."

My father smiles. "Alright," he says. We start toward the rock climbing wall, where barely anyone is at right now. Which is a good thing; I'll be able to do this in only a few minutes, and then we can move on to the rest of the rides.

I stare up and study the wall once we get to it. It's the perfect size for me. In fact, I think this is about the size of the rock wall I always climb at the beach. And, this one doesn't look like it'll be too easy either. It's tall and the footholds aren't placed in any exact pattern, so it'll be a little more difficult to get to the top. But I like that because I always like to challenge myself with things like this.

I get all strapped up and look up at the large wall again. I plan where I'll place my feet all the way to the top so I won't have to think about it as I go up, and then I finally start up the wall. The first part is easy, just like the rock wall at the beach, and the middle is where it gets a little harder. But it's not too bad; the footholds are just a little farther apart so all I have to do is stretch my feet a little farther. Once I'm past that, I find that the last part is just as easy as the first part, so I'm up to the top in no time.

I look down at my father, who's smiling at me from below. He seems so small from up here. In fact, everyone walking around down below seems small. I feel like I'm six years old again, at the top of this wall, smiling down at my parents from above. I wish my mother was here to see me do this again. I know what she'd look like if she was, though, so I just imagine that she's down there with my father, looking and smiling up at me like he is.

I look around at everything else from up here, since I like the view and I'm only going to be here for a few more seconds. I look at the ferris wheel and see that I'm almost level with the top of the ferris wheel from the height I'm at right now, but still just a little below. After taking in the view for a few more seconds, I finally let go and drop down to the ground safely.

I unstrap myself and head back over to my father standing a few feet away. He's still smiling at me.

"You've never lost your talent for rock climbing, have you," he says to me happily.

I shake my head proudly. "I've never stopped doing it," I tell him. "I love the feeling of getting to the top and seeing everything on the ground from up there."

"It is a great sight, isn't it?"

I nod and look up at the sky again. The sun had finished setting a little while ago, and it's started to get a bit darker now. Not much, but I can see a difference. I look back at my father.

"What now?" I ask.

My father shrugs. "Whatever you want," he tells me.

I look around us for anything that looks interesting. I point a little in the distance. "How about we go on that one?" I suggest. It's a relatively small ride, but most of the rides around here are like that. Nonetheless, they're just as fun as rides at a real amusement park, even if they're not as large.

"Alright," my father agrees. "There's a lot of rides like that in that area - let's go on all of them while we're at it."

"Okay," I say. I have no problem with that. Besides, all the lines are pretty short. We should be able to finish all of them by the time it gets dark.

Filled with anticipation and excitement, we start walking toward the rides.


It's about an hour later now, and my father and I are just getting off the last ride that we'd just gone on in this small little area. We'd gone on a few of the rides twice, but only the ones that had relatively short lines so we wouldn't have to wait too long.

The rides were amazing, just like I'd expected. My father and I had so much fun on all of them, especially the ones we liked so much that we'd done them twice. We exit out the gate of the last ride, and once we're outside my father looks at me.

"How'd you like those?" he asks me.

"I loved them," I say, grinning. "The last one was the best."

"It was," my father agrees. "That one really got a good scream out of us." He returns my smile.

It's true. We weren't expecting the last ride to be too bad, but it surprised us. It started out well, but it got crazy in the middle, and it caught us off guard for a few seconds since we didn't know it was leading up to that point at all. But that's what makes it fun.

It's definitely pretty dark now - finally the perfect time to go on the ferris wheel. It will be the last ride of the day, since my father and I are quite tired already after doing everything today, but I'm definitely not tired enough to skip the ferris wheel, especially since I've been waiting all day for this moment.

The line for the ferris wheel has shortened a great amount from how long it was before, but there are still some people waiting to go on it, probably the ones who had waited to do it until it got dark like us. We get into the back of the line and wait until they'll let us onto the ride.

Since this line isn't extremely long and the ferris wheel is big enough for a very large amount of people to get on at once, I'm assuming that everyone here will get to go when the people that are already on it get off. So we will probably only have to wait a little longer until we'll be able to get on.

Just as I suspected, a few more minutes later, the entering gate for us to walk through opens and the first few people walk inside. Of course, it will take a little while for everyone to take their seats because the wheel will have to keep turning until new seats are available for people to sit on all the way around. But after all the seats are filled, we'll finally be able to feel the amazing experience of what we've been waiting for so long.

Finally, when everyone is safely seated (surprisingly there are still a lot of empty seats), the ferris wheel starts turning and this time the ride starts for real. My father and I started closer to the ground since we were some of the last people in the line, and I stare at the world below as we slowly go up. When we first get to the highest point, I'm a little nervous since we're so high up, but I know I'm safe and there's nothing to worry about. And, at the same time, I can see almost the entire park from here. It's actually a little different from the view from the top of the rock climbing wall, because I really couldn't see *everything* from there. I could see a lot of the world down below, but I couldn't turn a full three hundred and sixty degrees to see every bit of it. And this is from a different point as well, which makes it even cooler.

We go around about four times, and we go around slowly, so there's time to really take in everything around you. I like to watch things go from big to small as we go up, and from small to big as we go back down again. And the way all the lights in the fair shine in the night is just a breathtaking sight to see. That was one of the things I was most looking forward to on this ride.

It takes about the same amount of time for everyone to get off the ride as it did to get on, and my father and I are one of the last people to get off. We exit behind everyone else through the gate at the other side of where we entered.

"That was amazing," I say to my father. "Even better than I imagined it."

"I think it might've been one of the best things we did here," my father says, smiling his warm smile. "It was definitely worth the wait."

It really was worth the wait. Everything else leading up to it was amazing as well, and I feel like we'd done everything in the perfect order. I smile to myself and I think about how amazing today had turned out to be.

The sky has taken on an even different color now, more toward a deeper, darker blue. It's started to get a little foggy too, which is unexpected, but it looks relatively clear against the darkness. At first, the fog was low, but it has lifted much higher above our heads since then. The stars have started to appear too, and I've been looking up at it all for a while now.

We walk over to the sidewalk in front of the park and wait for a taxi to pick us up and take us back home. Luckily, lunch didn't cost that much money, so we still have enough for the ride back to our house. Most of the people that had filled up the park earlier in the day have already left either recently or during the middle of the day, and we are one of the last few people here besides the ones who were running the events. Now that it's dark and the day is over, however, they've started taking the tents down and packing up, ready to go home and get a good night's rest. The park that was once lively and happy and filled with people during the day is now quiet and peaceful, so silent that I can hear a soft wisp of wind blowing small strands of hair across my face.

It's gotten noticeably colder in the past hour, and I wasn't wearing clothes that would necessarily keep me warm in this weather. Fortunately, the wind isn't too strong yet, and I'm thankful for that, but I'm also hoping we'll catch a taxi soon so we don't have to stand here for much longer.

I look down at my feet and keep moving my legs so I'm not standing so still that I feel colder than I want to. I hear people talking behind me - they must be some of the last people that were here with us until the end of the day.

Finally, I look up to the sound of screeching tires and see a taxi pull up right in front of us. The window rolls down and a man with a bushy gray beard pokes his head out. "Where to?" he asks.

My father leans over and tells the driver the address of our house. The driver leans back and considers for a second, then looks back and nods at my father. My father thanks him and and we walk around to the other side to get inside. We take the same seats as before: me in the back and my father in the front next to the driver. Once we've put our seatbelts on and we're set to go, the car begins moving. In a few seconds we turn at the corner of the street and the park disappears behind us.

I'm so exhausted that I have a feeling I may drift off right this second, but I know I have to stay up till we get home. So I just stare out the window like I usually do, watching. The bright glow from the street lights makes me squint and I'm tempted to close my eyes to avoid it, but I know I'll probably fall asleep if I do that, and I can't let myself do that yet. I'll be able to soon, and that's the only thing I'm looking forward to at the moment.

It's pitch black outside now, and I can't really see the fog anymore, even against the dark colors of the sky. I guess it must have cleared up.

What I can see is the stars, however. There are millions of them now, and I realize it looks exactly like someone had splattered white paint across a black canvas. The stars in the sky are shimmering too, and they're so bright I start to wonder if I'm seeing them differently because I never stare at the star-filled skies anymore, or if I just forgot how bright they are. Either way, I'm enjoying watching them now as they glitter in the night sky.

We turn onto another street. Since it's dark outside, it takes me a moment to realize that it's our street. We're home, and I sigh in relief.

Due to the fact that our house is at the top of the steep road, the driver parks right in front of our house at the top of the road, and we get out after my father pays the driver. I watch as the car drives out of sight, but it doesn't take that long because it disappears so quickly into the darkness.

I've gotten even sleepier, and now I can barely stand. I wobble on my feet as we walk up to the door. My father notices.

"Tired?" he asks me.

"Yes," I say groggily. "Today was a long, fun-filled day."

My father nods in agreement as he unlocks the front door. "Why don't you go right to bed then?" he suggests. "You seem like you need a good night's sleep."

I nod. "I'll see you in the morning," I say as I begin to walk inside. I turn back again for a second and say, "By the way, thank you for taking me today. The fair was the most fun I've had in a while. I had a great time."

My father smiles. "Of course. I had a great time, too. Goodnight."

"Goodnight."

I head up the stairs and only go to the bathroom before I decide I'm too tired to do anything else. I walk into my room and fall onto the soft, comfortable mattress and, before I know it, I've drifted off into the world of sleep and dreams.

• • •

In my dream, I'm standing in the middle of a grass field. It's a perfect grass field, however, with soft green grass perfectly cut and producing a fresh, wonderful smell. I look down to find myself standing in the field barefoot, and the gentle grass feels good under my feet. The sun is warm, but not scorching hot, which is a relief. The air is crisp, and it smells sweet, almost as marvelous as the smell of the grass.

I look around in all directions, realizing that there's probably no one else here for miles. It's just me.

I've started to walk now, and as I take small steps through the soft grass, I hear the faint chirping of birds above me. I look up to see a flock of them flying overhead in a large group. I watch them as they disappear from sight into the distance.

Then I hit something. I run into it, something hard and smooth. I stumble backwards and try to see what it is. I can't tell -

whatever I hit seems to be clear and translucent, for I can see right through it. It's like it's invisible, almost like there's nothing there in front of me, because I can't see it at all. But I know I definitely hit something, and I swear it felt like glass.

I walk a few steps closer and guide my arm up to feel whatever it was I ran into. My fingers touch something flat and solid and smooth, exactly like glass. It must be a large window or something; that's all I can think of it to be, at least.

I start walking to the right more, keeping my fingers trailing along the hard surface of the large window I hit. I want to see how high it goes, but due to the fact that I can't see it, it could go up as high as the sky for all I know.

As I keep walking to the right and continue to run my fingers over the glass, I wonder if this might go on forever in both directions. There's no end to it, which means I can't go any further past this point.

There's no point in continuing to walk, for I already know I can't keep going. As I look past the window, I realize there's no field stretching on beyond it. Looking behind me, I can see that nothing has changed there, but in front of me stands a forest, possibly filled with millions of trees and no sun. It's seems so dark in the forest, and I can barely see past the first few trees.

I don't know what to do. I don't want to go back yet. Besides, even if I do, where would I go? I don't even know how I got here in the first place, so I'm stuck. There was nowhere to go, nothing to do.

I suddenly hear the sound of rustling leaves in the distance. It's coming from inside the forest, as I soon realize. It must be a strong gust of wind or something making the leaves move, because there can't possibly be anyone on that side of the extensive window.

But I am wrong. A woman walks out from the trees, wearing a long white dress, although it seems it has become stained and dirty recently from the looks of it. The woman looks familiar.

It's my mother.

*No*, I tell myself. *It can't be.* It isn't possible for my mother to be here right now. She was gone.

The woman - my mother - sees me standing there, and begins walking toward me. I step back a few inches, scared. What if she's a ghost? What if she isn't real? If she's a ghost, she could walk right through the glass.

She looks real, however. She has my mother's eyes, and smile, and the exact same features. But if she's a ghost, she must be here for a reason, maybe to tell me something.

She walks up to me, and now she's right in front of me, but still on the opposite side of the glass barrier. She brings her hand up and places it on the glass, and I know what she wants me to do.

I do the same thing, until my hand is almost touching hers, but they are still separated by the glass. I feel like crying, for I'm so close to my mother but still so far away. I would do anything to be able to lock hands with her.

I can feel the tears in my eyes, but I keep them from spilling over. I see her start to fade away, like she is just mist. Her hand is still on the glass, and so is mine.

Before she is completely gone, I see her lips move. She mouths the words, *I love you*, and then she is gone.

The tears don't come, even though I thought they were going to. My hand is still on the glass where it has been ever since my mother's hand touched it on the other side.

And it stays there until I wake up.

*Chapter 4:*

*Hope Restored*


When I wake up, the first thing I see is the wall next to me. I stare at it for a few seconds, until the events of my dream suddenly come rushing back to me.

It's frightening how perfectly I remember everything that happened. I'm not sure how many hours went by after my mother faded away in my dream, or even if they were hours. Every detail is still so fresh in my mind that for all I know, I could've woken up minutes after the dream ended. Either way, I know I won't be able to get the dream off my mind for a while.

The main question that keeps repeating itself in my head is: What does it mean? It's all so confusing. I don't know why it's bothering me so much, because of course it is just a dream. But doesn't every dream occur for a reason? I feel like this one's important, and I don't think it's something I should ignore. Even though it wasn't real, it feels like it could be, and it doesn't seem like one of those random dreams. I know it means something, and I can't shake the nagging feeling inside me that I need to find out what it is.

There are millions of things the dream could have been telling me, so many I don't even know where to start. Could it have been telling me to never let go of my mother? Was it telling me to keep her with me wherever I go and wherever I end up in the future? Or was it just plainly reminding me of when I still used to have her with me? I don't know.

I swear I can still feel the tears that had filled my eyes in the dream, but they'd never spilled over. I'd never cried, not once. To be honest, I'm kind of surprised that I hadn't let myself cry. I should have, but I don't know what was holding me back. I guess

I was just so filled with shock that I'd been completely frozen, and it felt that way on the inside too. There were so many different emotions coursing through me that I don't even know how many there were. They were all feelings of surprise and sadness and regret and confusion, and I was experiencing them all at once, which made them kind of all combine into one big, single emotion. That's really the best way I can describe it.

I decide to let it go for now, because I know that if I keep thinking about it I'll never get it out of my mind. I know I'll figure it out soon, but for now I need to forget it and pretend it never happened. At least until I get some food in my stomach.

The dream starts to float to the back of my mind as the idea of food slowly replaces it. I realize just then how hungry I really am, and thinking about it more makes me even hungrier.

I sit up and throw the blankets off as I swing my legs off the edge of the bed. I look down to find myself in the clothes I wore to the fair with my father yesterday, and I'm confused for a second before I remember I'd never changed yesterday before bed since I was so tired. I decide I'll change after I eat breakfast. Once I'm out the door, I start for the stairs, but I stop halfway down the staircase as a strong, fragrant smell hits me.

It's coming from the kitchen, so I definitely know it's food, but I don't know what kind. I haven't smelled anything so good in a long time, and I wonder what's giving off such a wonderful scent. I hurry down the rest of the stairs and enter the kitchen. The smell gets stronger with each step I take toward the table.

Then I finally see where the delicious smell is coming from. There, on the table, is a plate filled with eggs, bacon, a few orange slices, and a piece of toast. Next to it is a tall glass of water, and in front of that sits a napkin with a fork and knife resting on top. My mouth falls open at the sight of it all.

My first thought is that my father must have made this for me. He doesn't seem to be in the house right now, however, so maybe he stepped out to get some groceries. I'm assuming he hadn't left too long ago, because the food seems to still be warm, otherwise it wouldn't be giving off such a delightful smell. Besides, I can still see the steam coming off of the eggs which, thankfully, means that everything is still fresh.

Before the food gets cold and my hunger gets any stronger, I walk over to the table and sit down in front of the food. I pick up the fork and knife and cut off a piece of the egg. Once I put the first bite in my mouth, I realize how much I've missed food like this.

I remember when my mother used to make this for me. She'd never make it too often, and when she did, she'd usually surprise me one morning like my father had done today. I remember how happy I used to be, and when she did prepare this for me, I'd always enjoy it slowly, knowing I wouldn't get it again for a while.

"Always take small bites," she used to say. "That way you'll be able to enjoy the taste in everything."

"But I'm so hungry," I used to tell her.

She'd smile and say, "If you eat too fast, it'll be gone before you know it. The flavor's stronger in smaller bites, and you'll appreciate it more."

I smile as I remember her saying that. I never eat anything so good too quickly anymore after what she'd told me, and I do indeed enjoy it more. My mother had always given me the best advice anyone could give, and it was one of the reasons everyone loved her so much. She won't be able to give me great advice again, but I'll always remember everything she'd told me in the past.

I finish the food in the plate and take a few long sips of water. After my mother died, I thought I'd never get anything like this again, but my father must have remembered how my mother used to make it for me - because I know he used to help her make it before - and he'd made it taste exactly the same. I can't wait until he gets home so I can tell him how thankful I am that he remembered.

I drink all the water in the glass slowly in the next few minutes and then lean back in my chair, stomach full and my hunger finally gone. I wonder what I'm going to do today, since I didn't have anything planned. I look out the window. It seems like a nice day from what I can see, a good day to spend outdoors.

The sound of the phone ringing interrupts my thoughts suddenly. I get up and quickly walk over to the other side of the kitchen where the phone is resting on the counter, pick it up and put it to my ear.

"Hello?" I say into the phone.

"Grace! I haven't heard your voice in such a long time!" someone exclaims on the other side of the line. I quickly recognize who it belongs to, and excitement rises up inside me. It's the familiar voice of my best friend, Sarah Matthews. I'd recognize it anywhere.

"Sarah?" I immediately ask. "It's been so long since I've talked to you."

"I know, I've missed you," says Sarah. "It's been almost two months since the last time I saw you."

"Yeah, it's been crazy lately," I say.

"Yeah," she agrees. "Everything with your mother, I'm assuming. I'm so sorry, Grace. I know how much she meant to you."

I sigh. "Thank you," I tell her. "That means a lot."

"Of course. But I was thinking if you're free, maybe you could come over today. We could spend the whole day together, maybe go down to the park, walk around and enjoy the perfect weather? We could use some time together since it's been a while." I can hear the smile in her voice, even through the phone.

I smile to myself. "That sounds great," I answer. "What time?"

"Well, now would be great if you can make it," Sarah tells me. "It's only noon. We have a couple hours to spend together before it gets dark."

"Okay," I agree. "I'll be there soon. Just meet you at your house first?"

"See you soon!"

She hangs up, and so do I, setting the phone back down where it was on the counter. I walk back over to the table and throw my napkin away. Then I pick up my plate, water glass, and the fork and knife, wash them in the sink, and then start back toward the stairs to head back to my room to change.

It doesn't take me long to pick what I want to wear. I choose a flowy white top and my usual pair of jeans, since I don't want to look like I just carelessly threw on some clothes without thinking about it. When I'm done changing I stand in front of the mirror and put my hair up in a fairly tight ponytail, making sure to smooth down all the strands of hair on my head and around my face so none will come loose. As soon as I've finished getting ready, I hurry back down the stairs. I remember to take some money and put it in my pocket for if we need to buy some food.

Once I've put my shoes on and I'm completely ready, I open the door and step outside, where I'm greeted by a soft, gentle breeze. I smile. The weather feels exactly the way I thought it would, with the sun warm, the blue sky absolutely clear and perfect, with not one cloud to be seen. And of course there's the breeze among it all, such a light wind that you can barely feel it. But it's there, and it balances everything out.

Sarah's house has always been in walking distance of mine, since we've both lived in the same houses all our lives. It's quite convenient, really, since when we do want to see each other it never takes too much effort to get to each other's houses. It's just a fifteen minute walk at the most.

I walk down the driveway and step onto the sidewalk. I quickly walk down to the road below, and wait until the cars stop and there's time for me to cross the road. I walk across the street to the other side, and once again review the way to Sarah's house inside my head, just to make sure I have it memorized. *Three more streets, turn left, and then two more streets,* I tell myself. Not too far away at all.

I keep walking. This street is completely shaded, the tall trees lining the sidewalk next to me providing a fair amount of protection from the sun. Since it isn't too hot even with the sun, I notice that it's actually a little chillier. But not too much that I actually feel *cold,* just a little cooler than the sun. Besides, the shade feels good in a way, too, so it's not too bad.

I reach the end of this street, and after I wait for the cars to pass again, I cross the road to the next one. Only a few more to go this way, then a couple more to the left, and I'll be at Sarah's house in no time.

I sigh and continue strolling down the street.

I'm lost in thought the rest of the way there, and I'm lucky to remember the way without directly thinking about it. I arrive at her house; it's at the top of a steep street just like mine is. I walk up to the front door and knock.

After a few seconds of waiting, I hear the click of a lock being turned, and the door is opened by Sarah's mother, who smiles in delight when she sees me.

"Grace!" she exclaims. "Why, we haven't seen you at all in the last few months. How have you been?"

"Good" I tell her. "I've been doing pretty well, and so is my father."

She nods. "Well, I'm very glad to hear that," she says. "I wouldn't be surprised if you two were a little shaky with.. well, you know, what's happened with your mother…" She trails off, and I can see she regrets bringing up the topic. Her expression has changed; she isn't smiling anymore. "Sorry," she says softly.

I don't mind. "No, it's okay. That definitely wasn't something we were ready for," I admit. "But it's gotten better, we've been okay, my father and I. More now than before."

"That's good," she tells me. "And… I'm so sorry… about the funeral…"

"No, no, it's fine," I assure her. "We know you wanted to come. It wasn't your fault." Sarah and her family hadn't been able to make it to my mother's funeral; Sarah was in Missouri with her father and her mother had been on a business trip. Of course, I'd been a little unhappy, but it wasn't intended for it to happen like that. We'd missed them, but it had been alright.

Sarah's mother smiles again. Then she changes the subject.

"So, what brings you here?" she asks me.

"Oh, well, Sarah asked me to come," I reply casually. "She called this morning."

"Oh, that's great," Sarah's mother says. "You two should spend some time together; it's been so long."

I nod in agreement.

"Well, I'll get Sarah; she's upstairs. She'll be delighted to see you."

I smile at her warmly. "Thank you," I say before she turns around.

"No problem," she replies. "Oh, and by the way, happy birthday. I know it's so late for me to tell you that; I'm sorry we couldn't tell you before - we weren't home that day."

"That's okay," I promise her. "Thank you though."

With that, she turns and half closes the door, leaving it open just slightly so it's not closed completely. I hear her footsteps fading as she walks away, and about a minute later I hear someone coming back to the door.

It swings open to reveal Sarah standing in the doorway. She has a wide grin on her face, and I'm assuming I do too.

"Hi," she says, coming outside to give me a tight hug. I hug her back, as tight as I can.

When she pulls away, the smile is still on her face. "I missed you so much," she tells me.

"I missed you too," I agree. "How are you?"

"I'm doing great!" she answers enthusiastically. "Everything's going well. How about you?"

"Pretty good," I tell her. "I'm doing well."

"That's good to hear," she says. "Well, are you ready to go?"

I nod. "Yep."

"Great." She closes the door behind her and I turn around as we start walking down the front porch steps.

"So how's it been?" I ask her. "You know, seeing your father a lot more."

Sarah looks at me. "Missouri's nice," she tells me. "I've seen a lot of it already - my father takes me places there when he's not at work. I like it a lot."

"That's good," I tell her happily.

"I used to miss him a lot," she goes on. "When I didn't see him as much. I was always with my mother, and even she would be gone most of the time. I was mostly alone for a while, until I started visiting my father in Missouri more often. I like it a lot better now that I can see both my parents."

I smile. "That's always a good thing. Being close to your parents is important."

"Yeah," she agrees. "I know how close you were with your mother. She was like a mother to me, too."

I give her a smile. "I know," I answer, with nothing but a little unease. "I miss her so much."

Usually, I get uncomfortable when people ask me questions about my mother now, but I don't mind it when it's Sarah. And even Sarah's mother asking didn't bother me much, due to the fact that I'm so close with them. I know they didn't bring it up to bother me. They aren't like that.

"It's harder to lose people when you're so close to them," she continues. "It makes the effect more painful and long-lasting. It must be terrible for you." She's been looking down for a while, but now she looks back at me. "I'm so sorry. Your mother should have been here longer. We all miss her so much."

I look back at her silently without saying anything. I can feel the emotion in her voice. In her words. Sarah's like me. She's empathetic. She and I have been that way; if anyone tells us anything that involves emotion and the way that they feel, we can understand almost exactly what they do. We've always been alike in that way.

It makes it easier to help people when you're empathetic to them, in a way, because you can get a good feeling of what they feel. She's not the one who lost my mother, but I can tell she knows the way I'm feeling about her death. It hurts her just as much as it hurts me, because she understands what I'm going through even though it hasn't happened to her.

"Thank you," I finally tell her. " I wish she'd been here longer, too. And don't feel bad about the funeral, by the way. It wasn't your fault you couldn't make it. I told your mother the same thing."

She nods and smiles. "We're getting closer to the park," she informs me. "We should be there soon."

"Okay." We keep walking, and then she speaks again.

"Do you want to get some ice cream?" she asks. "I know a really good ice cream shop by the park. Besides, it's about lunchtime, and if you're not too hungry, this will be a good snack."

"Yes, ice cream sounds great," I answer.

Sarah grins. "Good. You'll like this place."

I smile back. I remember how things used to be a long time ago. Memories come flooding back to me from those days, when I would walk to Sarah's house or she'd come to mine every day after school. Our favorite thing to do would be to go down to the park and play, and we'd stay there until the sun set and it started to get dark. I miss those days. Most of that is gone now, the times when I still had my mother and time to see Sarah every day. I'm not sure I'll be able to experience that the same way I used to again, no matter how much I want to.

And I do want to. Badly. I ache for the days when I had everything I wanted. I've never had a perfect life, but the life I am remembering now, the life I used to have, was as close to perfect as anything. It's all I wish for now, to go back. Maybe, if there was a way to go back, there was something we could've done to prevent my mother from getting cancer. Maybe then she'd still be alive now, and I'd still have her. It'd be like nothing had ever happened.

But I know that will never be possible, going back. No one can do that. I can guarantee that anyone else in the world that's going through the same thing as me wants exactly what I want, to go back. To change what happened. Maybe do something different, something that would stop whatever happened from happening. Or at least to try. Everyone deserves a second chance if they need it, but in these situations that chance will never come.

"This way," Sarah announces, pointing to the left. We turn and cross the street, and when we get to the other side I see that we're standing before a wide, long street with different shops and boutiques lining each side of it. I can see from here that each building is quite small, but there are many of them, all side by side to each other.

"The ice cream shop's one of these buildings," she tells me.

"We're almost there."

It doesn't take long before we find the shop; it's one of the smaller buildings among all of them, and it's very crowded. There are already too many people in line, so many that the line is still forming outside the building.

"How are there so many people here?" I ask Sarah curiously. "I've never seen a place this busy before."

She shrugs. "Maybe because it's a Saturday," she suggests. "And the weather's rare. It's a perfect day for ice cream."

"True," I agree.

"And believe it or not," Sarah continues, "this isn't the worst it gets. I've been here on a day where there's even more people - that's just how good the ice cream is. This is one of the best ice cream places you'll ever find around here."

"Wow, I didn't know it was *that* good," I say, grinning.

"It is, trust me," she promises me. "But the line goes by fast, don't worry."

I nod. We join the line behind the last person and wait. Indeed, as Sarah had said, we move up in the line fairly quickly until we finally make it through the doorway.

The inside of the building smells sweet. Like sugar. I take in the smell. Some people don't particularly like sweet scents like this, but I could breathe them in all day. It smells delicious to me.

We move up some more, and now I can see the glass case with all the ice cream flavors only a few steps ahead on our right. There are so many of them, and a lot of them are all my favorite flavors, which makes it hard to choose between all of them.

"Which flavor do you want?" Sarah asks as we move up a few more steps.

"Um, I think I'll get the mint chocolate chip flavor," I finally decide. "What about you?"

"Coffee," she instantly replies. "It's my favorite. And it's the best here."

I nod.

"Oh, do you have any money?" Sarah asks. "I forgot to ask you earlier."

I nod. "I remembered to take some before I left. I figured we'd get hungry and need to get some food while we're out."

Sarah smiles. "Good."

We're almost up to the counter now, and there are only a few people in front of us. I'm glad we didn't have to wait long. Even though I'd eaten a lot for breakfast, I'd gotten hungry fast. All that food must have gone through me quicker than I thought.

We wait behind the last people in front of us as they pay the man at the counter for their ice cream. The man looks young, and I assume he's probably in his early twenties. He hands them two medium-sized ice cream cones that are almost overflowing with ice cream, and they thank him and leave. I wonder how much ice cream a large cone would hold if a medium-sized one holds that much. Although, if this place is really as good as Sarah says it is, I probably won't have trouble finishing whatever amount of ice cream I get.

We're up next. Sarah steps forward and tells the man at the counter what we want. She gives him the money and I watch as he takes two ice cream cones from a stack on top of the glass case in front of us and puts a few scoops of ice cream inside each of them. After he fills them, he comes back over and gives them to us. We take them happily and thank him.

I see Sarah grinning as we walk back toward the door. She looks at me.

"Try it!" she urges. You'll love it."

I taste it. She's right.

"So...?" she asks hopefully.

"It's amazing," I tell her.

She nods, taking a bite of her own ice cream. "My mother and I come here sometimes," she explains. "On weekends when she's off work. We don't come all the time, but I get excited when we do. There's something different about this place. It's just... better."

"I'm enjoying it," I say happily. "Thanks."

"You're welcome," she answers warmly. "We should get to the park now. We can sit down for a little bit while we eat."

"Okay."

The park is only two or three blocks away from here, which is convenient since we don't have to walk too long to get there. We walk out of the ice cream shop and start heading back the way we came. I try not to eat my ice cream too fast without being so slow that it starts melting, and since there's so much of it, finishing it too quickly won't be a problem.

We're nearing the park now. I can see the large grassy field ahead of us, a couple trees here and there and stretching high up toward the sky, so high I can barely see the tops of some of them. I spot a park bench under a tree near a narrow pathway to the right of the field, and I can see from here that the large tree beside it casts a shade on the bench. I point to it in the distance.

"Do you think we should sit there?" I ask Sarah. "It's shaded, so we should be able to get some cool air."

"Yeah, that seems like a comfortable place to sit," Sarah says. We cross the street and begin walking over to the shaded park bench at the edge of the pathway. The first thing I feel when we walk under the tree is the refreshing breeze. It's amazing how different it feels in the shade than in the sun, even though there isn't as much sun today. I can still feel a difference.

"It's nice under here," Sarah comments, walking over to the bench to sit down.

I follow her. Sitting down by her side, I notice that I've finished about half of the ice cream by now. Not too bad. After all, there was a lot to begin with, so I'm eating at a reasonable pace.

"You know," I hear Sarah's voice, "we can come out here a lot more. To the ice cream shop, and the park. It's a fun place to hang out."

I nod as I turn toward her and take another bite of my ice cream cone. "I think that's a good idea," I agree gladly. "I like coming here."

"Remember when we used to come when we were little?" Sarah reminds me. Her expression tells me she's been thinking about it for a while, just like I have. "We came to this park together almost every day. There are a lot more trees now than before."

"I remember," I say. "And you're right about the trees. There were barely any a long time ago. It's nice though - everything's cooler under here."

Sarah smiles. "Yeah." She looks down for a second, then back up at me again. "When my parents divorced, and my father moved to Missouri, I used to come here often. I was a little younger, maybe ten or eleven. This was my safe place."

I listen to Sarah quietly, thinking about what she is saying. I don't think she's ever told me this, but I'm glad she's telling me now.

"I used to sit on one of these benches, right here," she continues, looking straight ahead as she keeps talking. "I would sit here and think. Let everything flow in and out of my mind, and I would try to figure it out, whatever was bothering me. But I eventually gave up. I realized that whatever happened has happened, and admitted that there was nothing I could do to change it."

I don't say anything as she explains, just continue to listen patiently. I know what she means. I am going through the same thing that she did a long time ago, but I know that even though she hadn't lost one of her parents, they'd separated, which may seem just as bad to her. And she was younger, which made it even harder. I know that I will eventually end up like her, the Sarah now, who has ultimately let go of those feelings. But I know it will take time. And however long it takes, I'm willing to live through it. Maybe it'll take only take a few months, or maybe it'll take years. But in the end, I'll finally reach what she has reached. What I've been longing for.

Happiness.

"Then I would just stare at the trees in front of me," Sarah goes on. "Watch as people walked by, walking their dogs or taking a jog or having a nice conversation with their partner. And I would let go of everything for a while, and I would appreciate everything around me: the trees, the breeze and the people around me, all of it." She pauses, and I can see she's thinking again for a second. "Then I would go home," she says. "Back to my mother. And we'd talk together for a while, about anything we wanted to. I'd try not to talk about my father, but sometimes it would come up. Otherwise we'd tell each other about anything that was on our minds, and we were happy like that."

I take in everything she just told me. Her words make me feel… confident, in a way. From what she's told me, and now that I'm letting what she said sink in, I don't quite feel as sad anymore.

"So, sitting on this bench in the park and watching everything around helped you take your mind off things," I say, looking at her.

She nods. "Yes. And I know it's hard now with your mother gone, but sometimes things like what I did can help you. Find a safe place like the park, and I guarantee it'll help you. It helped me, so I promise you that things will get better. Besides, you have your father. Talk to him as much as you can, like how I'd talked to my mother. Being honest with him will help you, and he'll understand you better if you tell him the truth. Trust me."

I do trust her. More than anyone. And I believe her. For the first time, I feel like the loss of my mother won't be the reason I won't make use of my life. It feels like an enormous load has been lifted off my chest. A load of sadness, regret, and the feeling that the rest of my life will be misery without my mother. But I know I will always remember her no matter what happens, and that's all I need. I can't live in sadness the rest of my life. There was a reason that what happened had happened. And although I may never know what that reason is, I'll be okay as long as I have her with me inside. I'll just have to keep telling myself that.

I look at her. "Thank you, Sarah."

"Anytime," she says. "And if you need anything, just come see me. I'll be at home for a while with my mother so I'm here if you need to talk."

I smile. "Thanks. I appreciate it. You don't know how much you've helped me."

"No problem," she answers. "I'm glad I did."

We finish the rest of our ice cream in silence. I listen to the birds and breeze as I sit there quietly eating my ice cream, enjoying the peacefulness. I've never felt so comfortable in a long time, and I feel especially pleasant now, after everything Sarah had just told me. I didn't know I'd be so deeply affected by what she said, but I felt like I could really understand her. It was almost as if I were her, because I could feel exactly what she was trying to say. Maybe that's just what it's like to be deeply touched by someone's words.

"So, do you want to walk around?" Sarah asks me. "Just for a little while, around the park."

"Yeah, that sounds great," I reply. We get up and walk across the rest of the field toward the pathway beyond it.

We walk in silence for a few minutes, and then I speak again.

"Do you miss your father?" I ask her. "You know, now that you're back with your mother again."

Sarah looks at me for a moment and then shrugs. "I guess I do," she replies. "After all, I'm not with my father as much as my mother, so I do wish I could see him more. But, I'm happy I do get to see him, at least, even if it's not for that long."

I nod. "How long were you in Missouri last month?"

"Two weeks I think," she answers. "It was a good amount of time I got to spend with him. That could've been the best time I've had out of all the times I've been there." I see the edges of her mouth turn into a slight smile.

"Well, I'm glad you got to spend time with him."

"Me too," she says.

"I went to the fair with my father yesterday," I tell her. "The one in the park downtown."

She grins at me. "Was it fun?"

"It was a lot of fun," I say. "Yesterday was the most time I've ever spent with my father since… well, since my mother died."

"Sounds like we both had a good time with our dads for a while," says Sarah. "Didn't you love to go to the fair when you were younger? That was all you'd talk about back then."

I smile. "You remember that?"

"Of course I do. How could I forget?"

"You're right," I agree. "When I was younger, the fair would be the one place I could really spend time with my parents. At least back then. And when I went with my father yesterday, it felt like how it used to feel, and I had a great time, even without my mother."

"I'm glad," Sarah tells me.

"I never thought that was possible either. For me to be okay doing something I used to enjoy doing with my mother. But I was okay. I missed her the whole time, but I was okay. I realized that I still had my father, and we had a great time."

"You're lucky you still have him," says Sarah. "You haven't lost everything. Your father still loves you, and that's the most important thing you need."

"I know," I reply.

She smiles at me in response.

• • •

It's a few hours later now, and it's getting closer to sunset. The sun isn't as warm as it was before and I can feel the air getting chillier as we walk. For the past few hours we'd walked around the park, had long conversations, and recently had just gotten some food since the ice cream definitely wasn't enough to fill us up. So far, this day is turning out to be just as fun as yesterday. Not that I thought it wouldn't be; I'm just glad Sarah and I have been having such a great time.

"It's getting colder," Sarah comments.

"I know," I reply. "But I have an idea."

Sarah looks at me. "What is it?" she asks eagerly.

"Well, the sun's about to set," I say. "We can go to the beach to watch it for a little while. It's not too cold yet. And besides, the sunset will be beautiful."

Sarah smiles. "Okay," she agrees. "I haven't watched the sunset in a long time. That'll be nice to see."

I nod in agreement, returning her smile. I know a perfect way to make watching the sunset even more enjoyable, and I can't wait to show it to Sarah.

By the time we get to the beach, the sun has barely started to set. We haven't missed too much of it yet, but I still want to hurry so we can watch the rest.

"Come on," I urge Sarah. We're still walking across the sand, and we're almost the other side. I point to the large wall of rocks that I'd climbed a few days ago. "We have to climb those," I say. "It's a perfect place to watch. Don't worry, it won't be too cold up there."

"All right," Sarah answers, grinning. I'm happy she's as excited about this as I am.

"Will your mother wonder where you are if we get back a little after dark?" I ask her. I don't want to keep her longer than she should be out.

Sarah shakes her head. "No, don't worry, my mother knows we haven't gone anywhere too far from home," she assures me. "What about your father?"

"No, he won't be worried either," I say. "We won't be back too late; maybe just as soon as it gets dark."

"Sounds good," says Sarah.

We reach the wall of rocks on the other side of the beach and I begin climbing up, remembering how I'd done it the last time I'd been here. Once I'd gotten to the top, Sarah begins climbing up after me, and I help her up once she's close enough. We sit down at the edge facing the ocean and the sun, and I realize we made it just in time.

I stare admiringly at the view before me. A sliver of the sun has just disappeared below the horizon, and there's still a good amount of time before the rest of it disappears. Even though it's so far away, it still seems so bright and radiant, almost more blinding than it is during the day. The sky is more of an orangish-pink now, and the color of the ocean seems a little darker than it usually is, but it all blends together to create one of the most beautiful things I've ever seen.

I look over to Sarah, who seems to be enjoying it as well. She looks back at me.

"Have you ever done this before?" she asks. "Watch the sunset from here?"

"Once," I reply. "When I was a couple years younger. I don't remember it too well, but I do remember that it was the first time I'd ever climbed up here. My father had taken me to the beach for a walk, and then we'd come up here together to watch the sunset."

Sarah nods. "Sounds nice," she says.

"I was probably too young to actually appreciate how beautiful everything was," I continue as Sarah listens. "I mean, I did think it was a pretty view and everything, but I don't think I knew how precious a view like this really is."

"I know what you mean," Sarah tells me. "I'll always remember this."

"Me too," I say.

After all, things like this are like photographs. Mental photographs, things that will be kept in your mind forever. Like this view. I will have two different memories of it now: the one with my father and now the one with Sarah. These memories will always be especially important to me.

Almost the entire sun has disappeared now, and the sky is even more orange than before. There's even a purple in the mix of all the colors, and still a little blue as well. I realize we picked one of the best days to watch the sunset.

I continue to stare at the sky in awe until I see the last sliver of the sun slip away out of sight. The sky still looks the same, but everything seems less bright all of a sudden. Now that the sun's gone, everything's darker. But the brighter colors that are still in the sky, like the orange and pink, still provide a little light, although not that much compared to how much light the sun gives off. But even though the sun's set, the view before us hasn't gotten any less stunning.

I look at Sarah after a few moments. "We should get back now," I tell her. "It's getting dark."

"Yeah," she says. "Before it gets too late."

We get up and climb back down the rock wall one by one

before starting to head back the way we came. I'm glad Sarah and I got to spend this day together. I'd missed her so much before I saw her today, and spending a whole day with my father and then a whole day with her had made my entire weekend so much better than I thought it would be.

We walk back up the steps once we get back to the other side of the beach and start back in the direction of home. It's a lot colder now, but luckily not cold enough to make us uncomfortable. It actually still feels nice, the weather, especially since the wind has died down.

"Thanks for showing me that," says Sarah, who is patiently walking beside me. "The sunset. I would've never thought something like that could be that amazing."

I nod. "You're welcome," I reply. "I think it was a good idea to watch that at the last minute. We'd made it just in time to see almost the whole thing."

"I wouldn't have missed something like that if I had the choice," she says. "I'll definitely be going back there once in awhile."

"So will I."

We cross the street. "Today was a great day," Sarah tells me.

"It was," I agree. "Thanks for calling me this morning."

She smiles.

I smile too.

I open the front door of my house and slowly walk inside. It feels as if in the last ten minutes the temperature had dropped several degrees and the wind had picked up quite quickly. I walk inside shivering from the cold, but the warmth of the house instantly starts to make me feel comfortable again.

I'd walked back to Sarah's house with her before heading back to my own, which added a bit of extra time to when I'd first planned to get back. But it was worth it; I couldn't have asked for a better day than today. Or yesterday, for that matter, when I'd spent the day with my father. I smile to myself for a second before I start making my way to the kitchen.

I see my father at the dining table, already eating dinner. I walk across the kitchen over to him, and he looks up at me.

"Look who's finally back," says my father with a grin as I sit down in the chair next to him. "How was your day?"

"It was amazing," I tell him, smiling. "I spent the day with Sarah."

"Sarah?" he repeats, surprised. "It had been so long since you'd last seen her, right?"

I nod. "Almost too long," I agree. "She'd called this morning to ask me to come over. We went down to the park together, and we got ice cream on the way, too. We even watched the sunset from the beach."

"Sounds fun," my father comments. "Was the sunset nice?"

"It was beautiful," I reply. "One of the most amazing ones I've ever seen. It reminded me of the time you took me to see the sunset from that beach a few years ago."

My father nods. "I'll never forget that day," he says. "It was the first time you'd ever seen the sunset from that beach."

"Really?" I ask. "I thought I'd been to that beach before that."

"You had, but you'd never watched the sunset from there until that day," he explains. "You were so happy. You'd point off into the distance at the sun, and tell me how bright it was. And you'd tell me how blue the ocean was. And how many colors the sky had in it. Even when you were so young, you were so observant. You still are."

I'm smiling even wider now. I love when people tell me about the times I was younger. It's fun to listen to those stories, especially when your parents are telling you them, and I love remembering all the great memories within them. Sometimes you never realize the similarities between you and your younger self until you listen to stories about your past.

"Thank you," I say to my father. "And thanks for the breakfast you made for me this morning," I add, remembering again how delicious the food had tasted.

"You liked it?"

"I loved it. It tasted just like how Mom made it."

"Good," he says. "I'm glad you enjoyed it."

"Me too," I agree.

"By the way, if you want some dinner, there's soup in that pot on the stove over there. There's still quite a bit in there for you, if you're hungry. It's your favorite - tomato soup."

"Okay," I say, getting up. I'm not starving, since Sarah and I got food only a little while ago, but I could definitely still eat. Especially my favorite tomato soup, because there's no way I can resist it, no matter how full I am.

I walk over to the stove and grab a bowl first from one of the cupboards above me. Also making sure to grab a spoon, I scoop some of the soup from the pot into the bowl until it's about half full. I don't want to take too much at first, since I can always get more later.

I take the bowl of soup back to the table and sit down to eat. I take a spoonful of the warm liquid and put it to my lips. No one would ever expect that something so thin would have so much flavor, but this does. It tastes so good that with each bite I take, I get even hungrier, until I finally finish all the soup inside the bowl.

"Full?" asks my father.

"Nope," I say with a grin as I stand to fill up my bowl again. I've never been able to get enough of this soup, or anything my parents make for that matter. I love eating out at restaurants once in a while too, but in the end I always find myself enjoying my parents' food more. It's always been that way, and I think it's great because it means I'll never get tired of eating it.

"So, Grace," says my father slowly as I sit back down to start eating again. "There's something I need to talk to you about."

I look up at him. There's something about his tone, something that tells me he's doubting what he's about to say. "Is it something bad?" I ask with a frown, the curiosity showing in my voice.

My father hesitates. "It's good and bad," he tells me. "Well, not really bad, unless you think of it as bad."

"Start with the good news then," I tell him as I put another large spoonful of soup to my lips.

"Well, I had a job interview a few days ago," begins my father.

I raise my eyebrows at him, hope and excitement already starting to rise inside me. "And?"

"They offered me the job!"

My mouth drops. "Really? That's amazing!"

"I'm excited too," my father agrees.

"What's bad about that?" I ask, remembering that my father had said that there was bad news.

My father hesitates again. "Well…"

"What is it?"

"My job is in New York."

The words spill out of his mouth so fast as if they're water.

I'm not sure if I heard him correctly. "What? New York?"

My father nods. "Yes, New York."

"Did you know about this before they offered you the job?" I ask.

He nods again. "I didn't tell you because I still didn't know if they were going to offer me the job. But I think I'm going to take it."

There are so many emotions and thoughts running through my head that I don't even know what to say. I'm still trying to process the information, and there's this pit starting to form in my stomach that I can't seem to get rid of.

"You're going to take it?" I finally manage to get out. "We're… going to have to move to New York."

"I know," my father says. "But we both know we need the money, and after what happened with your mother, we need to take anything we can get. And luckily, this isn't something bad that we're going to need to settle for. I haven't had any good job offers until now, and this is a really good one. I'll get paid well, and I won't have to work so often that I'll never get to see you. It'll be perfect."

*Maybe it will be,* I think to myself. Except for the fact that we're going to have to leave this place. This is where I've lived my whole life. Where I've grown up. Where all my childhood memories are. Where I met Sarah. Where I can go to the beach every single day and enjoy the amazing peacefulness of the world around me. This is my *home*. I'm not ready to leave yet.

"I can't," I tell my father. "I can't just pick up and forget every-thing that's happened here, which is, by the way, my entire life. And there's absolutely no way I can leave Sarah. She's my closest friend, practically my family. And New York is so different. Differ-ent lifestyle, different people, different weather, different every-thing. It'll be so hard to adjust to all that."

"You're not the only one that is taking this so hard," my father tries to assure me. "Believe me, this is not easy for me either. You think I want to leave? This is my home too. I love this place. But we really don't have a choice. If I don't take this, I really don't know how we're going to manage even having a home any longer. Taking or not taking this job isn't going to change how hard the next few months of our life are going to be. I know it's going to be difficult to leave, but pretty soon, New York will become our home too."

"But I'm not ready!" I say, not realizing my voice has been get-ting higher and higher with everything I say. "I can't leave."

"Grace," says my father. I can tell he's trying his best to stay calm. "We don't have any other choice. It's the best thing for us at this point. We can't afford to pass up this opportunity."

I want to yell more, keep saying the same things and try to con-vince my father that we can't leave. But there's definitely truth to his words. And I can't deny that. As hard as it is, I have to admit that what he's saying isn't wrong, and we definitely do need it at this point. The pit in my stomach is getting larger and larger, and by now I feel so empty inside I don't even know what to do. I know that nothing I say will change my father's decision, so what's the point in wasting my breath?

I just nod, and eat the rest of my food in silence.


The day is here.

It's been a week since I found out about my father's new job. I'm sitting in my room on my bed, thinking. I still can't believe that these are the last few minutes I'll be in this house.

My father and I have been trying to make the last few days in our home as memorable as we could make them. We went all over town doing our favorite things, and as we did them so many old memories came back to me and made me and my father smile. It also made me a little sad that I won't be able to do all those great things anymore, but I've been trying to push those feelings away and focus on this new chapter in my life.

I had also called Sarah a few days ago to tell her about the news. It was really hard for me; I remember there were times where I was so close to crying because I didn't know what it was going to be like leaving her. I could tell from her voice that she was on the verge of crying as well, and that she was taking this news just as hard as I had. She had told me that it was going to be okay in a little while though, and that we could always talk on the phone whenever we had time. I agreed, and I convinced myself that even though it was going to be so different, I wasn't losing Sarah for-ever.

She had called earlier today to wish my father and I a safe flight, and that she was going to miss us so much. I told her I was going to miss her too, but that we'll try to visit when we can.

"Five minutes!" I hear my father call from downstairs, warning me that the taxi will be here shortly. His voice snaps me out of my thoughts and back to reality.

I jump off my bed and walk over to the mirror to fix my hair quickly before we have to go. I stand there for a little while as I re-member what Sarah said at the park a while ago about how every-thing with the loss of my mother will get better. I really felt her words at that moment, but I lost a little hope when I found out I'd be leaving Sarah as well.

But as I look in the mirror, I forget all my bad feelings. All of a sudden, I see my mother. She's my reflection in the mirror. She smiles at me, my favorite warm, loving smile, and it makes me smile back at her. And then I see me in the mirror again - my actual reflection.

And that's that point of realization for me. When I really feel and understand Sarah's words again, but even more this time. My mother was never gone. Well, she was, physically, but not completely. Her spirit was inside of *me*. She's always been in my heart. Even when she was alive. I never really lost her. And this is the moment that I really, truly believe that.

I smile to myself again. Suddenly, I'm not dreading this anymore. My father and Sarah were right. I know that this will be hard. But I'm not going to let it affect me anymore. My mother taught me to make the best out of any situation that gets thrown my way. This is one of those situations, and I need to take her advice and make the best of it. I take another deep breath.

I begin walking out of my room, but before I close the door I look back one more time. I look at it for a few seconds just to remember it, and then I finally close the door and start heading toward the stairs.

I walk over to my father downstairs, who is standing beside the door with all our bags and suitcases.

"The taxi's here," he tells me. "Are you ready?"

I grin.

"Ready."